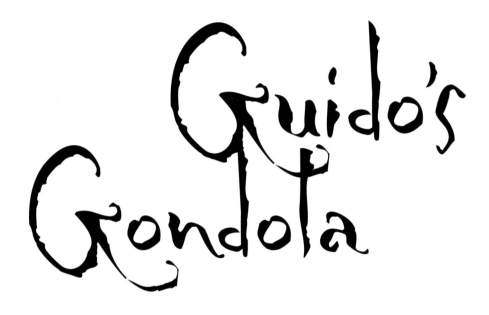

Guido's Gondola

by Renee Riva

illustrated by Steve Björkman

WATERBROOK
PRESS

GUIDO'S GONDOLA
PUBLISHED BY WATERBROOK PRESS
2375 Telstar Drive, Suite 160
Colorado Springs, Colorado 80920
A division of Random House, Inc.

Scripture taken from the *Holy Bible, New International Version*®. NIV®. Copyright © 1973, 1978, 1984 by International Bible Society. Used by permission of Zondervan Publishing House. All rights reserved.

ISBN 1-4000-7060-0

Text copyright © 2005 by Renee Riva

Illustrations copyright © 2005 by Steve Björkman

Library of Congress Cataloging-in-Publication Data
Riva, Renee.
 Guido's gondola / by Renee Riva ; illustrated by Steve Björkman.— 1st ed.
  p. cm.
 Summary: Guido, a young rat, loves giving tourists rides in his small gondola in Venice, Italy, until he is persuaded to add a motor, then buy a large boat, then an even larger one, until he realizes he misses the small things in life.
 ISBN 1-4000-7060-0
 [1. Boats and boating—Fiction. 2. Belongings, Personal—Fiction. 3. Contentment—Fiction. 4. Rats—Fiction. 5. Venice (Italy)—Fiction. 6. Italy—Fiction. 7. Stories in rhyme.] I. Björkman, Steve, ill. II. Title.
 PZ8.3.R523Gu 2005
 [E]—dc22

                                                      2004018613

Printed in Mexico
2005—First Edition

10 9 8 7 6 5 4 3 2 1

To my mom and dad,

who taught me that if you shoot for the stars,

you'll at least hit the moon.

Better one handful with tranquility

than two handfuls with toil

and chasing after the wind.

ECCLESIASTES 4:6

Near an old pier in Venice,
where small children play,
Guido's gondola
ferried tourists each day.

The young rat enjoyed
the tourism trade,
rowing at noon
with a breeze in the shade.

Along Lover's Lane
the gondola swayed,
carrying sweethearts
as soft music played.

With rides so romantic,
charming, and quaint,
tourists loved Guido
and thought him a saint.

Gracious and helpful,
yet light as a feather,
Kids feared he might
blow away in bad weather.

But Guido's big heart
made up for his size.
He was tremendous
in everyone's eyes.

One day he stopped
to pick up a client,
who climbed aboard
with trunks that were giant.

"A motor," the man said. "That's what you need,
to make your job easy and give your boat speed."

"Your life will be better. Business will grow.
Think of the time that it takes you to row!"

That night Guido drifted beneath a bright moon
to sweet serenades from a faraway tune.

In the morning he arose with one thought in mind:
"A motor?" he wondered. "Perhaps it is time."

He picked out a motor of fireball red,
then changed his mind for a blue one instead.

The man had been right
in the rightest way.
The new speedboat business
increased each day.

So many people!
So much stuff to tote!
Guido worked fast
with his super speedboat!

One day a rather large
woman climbed in
with two chubby children
and one who was thin.

She worried the speedboat
might not stay afloat,
"What you need, my dear,
is a much bigger boat."

That night 'neath a wondrous, star-studded sky,
Guido's gondola puttered on by.

But the next morning with ink on his tail,
he painted a sign that said, "BOAT 4 SALE."

It didn't take long
for the speedboat to sell.
It had, after all,
been cared for quite well.

Guido's new yacht was
stunning and stellar,
with big jet engines
and a turbo propeller.

Guido gave tours
and found it quite funny
that folks were so happy
to pay him big money.

Just when he thought
he had almost enough,
a man came aboard
with way too much stuff.

"I have an offer.
To be quite specific,
I'll pay you to ship it
to the Pacific."

Guido set sail on a much larger ship,
while his poor little yacht went to her slip.

The first day at sea
his spirits just soared.
The second day out,
he felt a bit bored.

He laid on the deck, just sunning his tail
'til the wind turned to a blustery gale.

The winds and the rains continued for weeks.
He was chilled to the bone, with little chapped cheeks.

One long, dark night
as he nibbled on toast,
he suddenly realized
what mattered most.

It wasn't the boat
or stuff that he had.
The small things in life
were what made him glad.

He missed the music,
the soft serenade,
singing to sweethearts
adrift in the shade.

He yelled from the deck,
"Enough is enough!
It is not all about
big boats and stuff!"

True to his word
he completed his trip,
then sailed back home
on his big empty ship.

That evening 'neath a glorious,
warm summer sky,
a little gondola
zipped quickly by.

Dear Guido's sad heart
filled up with great joy.
"Excuse me, young lad,"
he called to the boy.

"I'll swap you my ship
if you'll come ashore.
Keep the blue motor,
just leave me the oar!"

To this day in Venice where children still play,

a very wise rat ferries tourists each day.

Each evening at twilight beneath a bright moon,
his gondola sways to a faraway tune.